15/20.   TEN

WITHDRAWN

Books should be returned or renewed by the last
date above. Renew by phone **03000 41 31 31** or
online *www.kent.gov.uk/libs*

THE GOODY

ORCHARD

lauren child

For Lucy Lardle,
the goodest Goody

ORCHARD BOOKS
First published in Great Britain in 2020
by The Watts Publishing Group

1 3 5 7 9 10 8 6 4 2

Text and illustrations © Lauren Child, 2020

A CIP catalogue record for this book is available
from the British Library.   ISBN 978 1 40834 758 4
Printed and bound in China.

Orchard Books   An imprint of Hachette Children's Group
Part of The Watts Publishing Group Limited
Carmelite House, 50 Victoria Embankment, London, EC4Y 0DZ
An Hachette UK Company
www.hachette.co.uk
www.hachettechildrens.co.uk

Chirton Krauss was a good child, the very goodest.
He did everything he was told, when he was told.
He even did good things *without* being told.

That's how good he was.

Chirton always ate his broccoli, every single stalk,
    even though broccoli was his least favourite of all his least favourite vegetables.

He washed his hands after every little trip to the small room.

And, of course, he always used soap.

He didn't just wet his fingers under the tap like some people do.

He always went to bed exactly on time.
He never argued and he never whined.

Bedtime *is* bedtime, after all,
don't you agree?

He never, ever stuck his finger up his nose.

Not even when he was absolutely certain
that no one was looking.

And he always made sure that the rabbit's hutch was cleaned out once a week –
even though his sister Myrtle was meant to do it every other Friday.

Somehow she always forgot.

But Chirton Krauss didn't mind one bit because he loved the rabbit,
and most importantly he was
The Goody.

Being good, after all, *is* very important – isn't it?

Well, Chirton's parents thought so. In fact, they had given him a Goody Badge,
just in case he ever forgot what a good child he was.
They did not want him to forget, ever.

If people have decided you are good, do not disappoint them by being bad.

Chirton's sister, Myrtle, had never been given a Goody anything.
Not *even* one of those goody bags they give out at the end of a party.

Myrtle wasn't invited to parties any more.

You see, Myrtle was not a good child, everyone told her so.

And Myrtle never forgot to remember this.

If people have decided you are bad, do not disappoint them by being good.

And so things continued until one lunchtime. Chirton was struggling with his broccoli when a thought occurred to him. "Why doesn't Myrtle have to eat broccoli?"

"Because Myrtle won't," said his father. "Poor Myrtle isn't a Goody and doesn't understand how *important* it is to eat vegetables she doesn't like."

Yes, poor Myrtle, that is sad.

The next week, when Chirton was cleaning out the rabbit for the forty-third Friday in a row, he said, "Why doesn't Myrtle ever clean out the rabbit's hutch?"

"I have given up reminding her," said his mother.
"It's lucky that you are a Goody and will do it for her."

That *is* lucky, isn't it?

A few nights later, Chirton woke up with a tickly cough, so he went downstairs to get a glass of water.

He found Myrtle watching TV and stuffing choco puffs into her mouth.

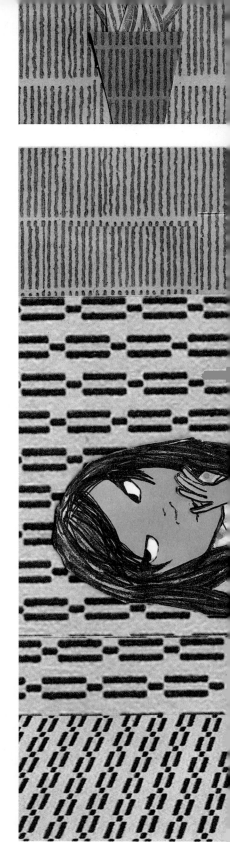

She wasn't eating them carefully — a lot of them were going on the carpet.

"How come Myrtle is allowed to stay up late watching TV?" asked Chirton.

"Oh, I can never get Myrtle to go to bed," said Alba, the babysitter. "So I just let her stay up."

Now . . . does that sound fair to you?

Chirton went back upstairs but he could not sleep, his head was too full of thoughts. He was thinking:

"*I* would quite like to stay up LATE watching TELEVISION and eating CHOCO PUFFS. Why is it always ME who has to CLEAN OUT the rabbit? I HATE broccoli."

Most of all, he was thinking:

"What is so GOOD about being a Goody?"

You were probably thinking this some time ago.

The following day, Chirton Krauss did not wash his hands when he went to the toilet and he did not eat his broccoli at suppertime.

Nor did he clean out the rabbit on Friday.

And why should he?

"But you have to clean the rabbit out because I always forget," said Myrtle.
"You are The Goody, everyone expects you to be good."

At bedtime, Chirton made a horrible fuss and got up several times to get snacks.

Alba looked anxious. "Please be good," she begged.

Alba's eyes went a bit watery and Chirton felt a funny, heavy feeling in his tummy.

Was it the choco puffs?

When Chirton's parents got home, they were very disappointed.
"But I want to be BAD like Myrtle," said Chirton.

"Goodies do NOT get other people into trouble," said Myrtle.

Chirton unpinned his Goody Badge and stamped on it until it was flat.

The next morning, Chirton was not allowed to go to Lara Perella's birthday party.
Lara was new to the neighbourhood and Chirton very much wanted to be friends.

He had made her a special card to say so.

Myrtle was sent to deliver it.

Lara didn't know about Myrtle being bad, so she invited her to stay for the party.
And Myrtle did – right until the end.

She even got a goody bag.

It was a good feeling to go home with something.

Chirton did not feel good. His tummy was still heavy, so he went to see the rabbit.

He thought watching it hop would make him feel better.

But the rabbit was not hopping. There was no room for hopping.

So Chirton cleaned the hutch, and when he did the rabbit seemed to smile.

Can rabbits smile?

When Myrtle came home she said,
"You cleaned out the rabbit, even though it was my turn to do it for the last twenty-three weeks. Thank you, Chirton."

Can Myrtles say thank you?

"You should have the goody bag," said Myrtle.

"That's nice of you," said Chirton.

"Well, you *are* The Goody," said Myrtle.
"You did clean out the rabbit hutch."

"I didn't do it to be a Goody," said Chirton.
"I did it because the rabbit likes to hop."

And Chirton thought about that
because it was true:

"Being a Goody is not what makes you nice.
    But being nice when you can be nice
        can make you feel good."

So they shared the goody bag,
    and Chirton's heavy tummy feeling
            COMPLETELY disappeared.

Sharing has a way of making you feel better.

That dinner time, Myrtle announced,
"Chirton does not like broccoli."

"I know that," said their mother.
"But he eats it anyway because
he has *always* been The Goody."

"And you don't because you are not,"
said their father.

"NEITHER of us are Goodies,"
said Chirton.

"And neither of us are not Goodies,"
said Myrtle. "And people do not
always have to eat broccoli,
not if they really hate it."

Quite right, no Goody would
ever expect them to.

So they gave the broccoli to the rabbit instead.
And the rabbit seemed to smile because it was very fond of broccoli.

Can rabbits smile?

Chirton and Myrtle's parents
decided to stop being disappointed,
because although sometimes
Myrtle was bad and occasionally
she was very bad . . .

mostly she tried to be nice, and
that was the important thing.

Trying is much better than not trying,
don't you think?

And sometimes Chirton was good and sometimes he was less good
and occasionally he wasn't good at all.
        But his parents always appreciated it when he was.

Being appreciated is very important, isn't it.